His Dirty Secret

Book 3

Mia Black

Table of Contents

Chapter 1

Jayla

I was racing to the hospital. I had to go see Keon. Tiana was too hysterical on the phone. After she told me that our brother was shot, she just broke down in tears. I couldn't get any answers from her, so I just hopped in my car and made my way to the hospital.

This was my worst fear. For the longest time, I'd been telling Keon that this could be his fate. One day he was going to bump into the wrong person at the wrong time. He always said that it was all in my head or that I was making it up, but now look. I didn't want to be right. I was hoping that maybe with Darius as a good influence in his life, maybe if he tried to be like Darius, he would turn his life around, but I guess it was too little too late.

I'd been trying to reach Keon, but everything was going to voicemail. I got so desperate that I was calling his knucklehead friends. I knew one of them had to know what was going on with Keon. I just needed something. I just needed an update on Keon. I didn't want to get to the hospital and be surprised. I didn't want to be floored with the news. Every one of his friends either let the phone go to voice mail or ignored my call. I was being kept in the dark. That can't be good news.

I parked my car not far from the hospital. As soon as I got into the hospital, I went straight to the desk.

"Miss, I need information on Keon Simmons. He was just brought in here."

"Hold on one second."

"Hold on?" I rolled my eyes. "Bitch, did you hear what the fuck I just said? Stop with the bullshit and just give me the information that I need."

"Miss, if you would just—"

"No. If you would just look up the information, I will be out of your way. All of this back and forth between me and you is really unnecessary."

"No. What is unnecessary—" She started to raise up from her seat. It's about to get real in here.

"Lanae, just give the woman the information," the security guard said. "I'm not breaking up no fight over bullshit." He took a sip from the bottle of water he was holding. She slowly sat back down and began typing on the computer. I looked at this woman before me. She was just about my age, but she had ten different colors in her hair. Now having color in your hair was cute, but not when there was so many and they didn't even compliment you. She wasn't trying to be professional, and seeing how she was about to go toe-to-toe with me, she wasn't being professional either.

"Keon Simmons has just been transferred to room S408." She still had an attitude, but at least she was doing her job. "May I please have your ID?" I dug into my purse. I should fling it at her ass, but if she was cooperating, I needed to as well.

"Here you are," I said as politely as I could. She pulled out a visitor's pass and wrote my name on it. "I wrote the room number on it. You take the elevator that's down there to the left to the fourth floor." She didn't look up at me and practically waved me off, but I had bigger things to do.

The walk to get to Keon's room was like a journey. I didn't know what I was going to see. Maybe if I hadn't got an attitude with the front desk attendant, I might have gotten more information out of her. I guess when she gave me a little bit of trouble, I released all of my anger on her. It wasn't right, I knew that, but I was going crazy here. I could be walking into this room and find my brother brain dead or hooked up to a bunch of wires or missing limbs. Who knows what I would see as I opened this door?

"Hey sis." Keon was sitting upright on the bed, looking like his normal self. I had to blink twice to make sure that I wasn't seeing things. Maybe I just wanted him to be well so bad that I was making this up. Nope. He looked like he was fine.

"They told me you were shot." I sat down on the seat that was next to the hospital bed. "I thought you were shot."

"I am Jayla." He lifted up his right arm as much as he could. His face scrunched up a little, so I knew he was in a little bit of pain. "I was shot in my arm."

"What the heck is going on Keon?"

"What?" He shrugged his shoulders.

"No! No. You're not going to do that. You're not going to try to play it off like nothing serious happened. You're going to tell me what happened." He looked at me like I was playing a joke or something. "I'm waiting." I crossed my arms.

"Fine. If that's what you want." He started. "I was just hanging out with my boys by his house. We were just sitting outside when this dude rolled up in his car. Malik, you know him?" he asked me, and I just nodded my head. Malik was one of his knuckleheaded friends, but to be honest, there were so many, I was losing count.

"Yeah. So they start getting into it, and next thing I know, he pulls out and starts shooting."

"Just like that."

"Just like that."

"And you didn't do anything?"

"Why you gotta do that Jay? Why you gotta make it my fault?"

"I just don't get how somebody could just start shooting at you if you didn't do anything."

"That's how it is in the streets sometimes."

"And that's why I want your ass to stay out of them."

The room got quiet. I could see Keon's mind racing. It was almost as if he was looking for something to say back to me. We were always going back and forth, but I think that this bullet finally brought my message loud and clear. Who knew all it took was him getting shot for him to actually think about what I was always telling him?

"How is my patient doing?" A man came walking in. Since he had a stethoscope and a white jacket, I guessed he was the doctor.

"I'm okay," Keon answered.

"I'm his sister. What can you tell me about his injuries?"

"Well, your brother was shot by one bullet, and lucky for him it didn't hit anything. All I had to do was take the bullet out, patch him up, and send him up here. He should be fine."

"Thank you." I sighed in relief.

"Now, I don't want to make it sound like it is going to be easy, but he shouldn't be home alone. He's going to need as much help as he can get. Although it was a lucky shot, that doesn't mean he can take it easy. He cannot move that arm at all. It needs to heal properly. In order for his arm to heal properly, he can not move it at all."

"Don't worry, he's going to be staying with me." I shot Keon a look. I didn't need him trying to talk back now. He's going to be staying with me whether he liked it or not.

"That's perfect. That's actually what he needs. He needs to be taking it easy." The doctor smiled.

The doctor then checked on his arm. When Keon moaned a bit in pain, he gave him some medication.

After the doctor was finished with the checkup, he turned back to me.

"The way your brother's injuries are looking, he may get discharged soon. You just make sure that he takes it easy, takes the pain meds when he needs them, and never moves that arm."

"Absolutely." I smiled more after hearing the good news.

When he left, Keon started to open his mouth, but I shut him down.

"Nope." I cut him off.

"You don't even know what I'm going to say."

"I don't really care. You are staying with me full time. There is going to be no more of you running in and out bullshit. I'll get you some things for the condo, and you're staying with me, period." I crossed my arms. It was the end of the conversation. Keon was going to stay with me. I was going to get him on the right track, even if it killed me.

Two weeks flew by like it was hours. I guess I was just anxious for Keon to come home. After his wound healed up enough, the doctor let him go. His doctor made sure to tell us again that Keon should take it easy. We agreed, and when we got outside, I expected to see Darius. I hadn't seen him a lot because I've been by Keon's side the whole time. He sent me messages to keep my head up, and when I told him that we were getting out today, he offered to pick us up.

"Where's your car?" Keon asked as the doctor and nurse left. I kept looking around for Darius or even his car. When I texted him last night, he told me for sure that he was coming, but it looked like something had come up.

"Something is wrong with it," I lied, looking at my phone. Nope, there were no text messages from him at all. "I'm getting us a cab." I smiled but I wanted to cry.

"It should be here any minute." I said, as I was already getting us an Uber.

"Maybe I'll have one of my friends look at the car," Keon suggested.

"No. It's cool."

"Hmm, ok." Keon added.

"What's that supposed to mean?" I snapped back.

"You don't think I know game when I see it?" He revealed.

"What you mean?"

"I know we over here waiting for that nigga you been fucking." His eyes narrowed. "I bet you that he said that he will pick us up, huh?"

"No," I lied.

"Whatever J." He rolled his eyes.

I would have continued the argument, but luckily the Uber came up then. I helped him inside and then went in the other door. I gave my directions to the driver and leaned back into the seat. The whole cab ride there was awkwardly quiet. Keon kept looking over at me, but I didn't really make eye contact with him. I didn't want to face the fact that he might be telling the truth about Darius.

When we got home, Keon took his pain pills and went straight to sleep. I tried calling Darius, but his phone was off. I wanted to think more about it, but I just went to bed. I tossed and turned for a while and eventually fell asleep.

The next morning I decided to start the day fresh. I wanted Keon to feel as great as he could, so I made a huge breakfast. I made chocolate chip pancakes, fried up some bacon, sliced up fruit, made hash browns, and I juiced up some oranges. Cooking a huge breakfast like this reminded me of old times. I used to make a huge breakfast like this for Tiana and Keon at least once, every Sunday. Keon would come in running, going straight for the bacon. Tiana would come down, and depending on her mood, it was either eggs or just fruit. We would all just eat and catch up. It'd been years since we'd been like that.

"Damn, what's that smell?" Keon yawned, walking in. "I haven't smelled nothing this good in a minute. Tell me that you made the pancakes the way I like."

"You mean with a little touch of vanilla?"

"Yes!" His eyes got wide and bright. "You remember after all this time?"

"Of course I remember Big Head." I stuck out my tongue at him. "You're my brother. I used to make this for you and Tiana back in the day. You used to be so greedy."

"I wasn't greedy."

"You would go back for seconds, thirds, and fourths. Do you know that you are the reason that when I cook breakfast, I almost always make too much? I had to teach myself how to make breakfast for one."

"Really?" He was laughing, and I joined along with him. "Well, no one has managed to make a breakfast like this." He continued.

"Not even all those sluts you've been sleeping with?" I gave him a slick smile.

"Oh, ha ha." He laughed back sarcastically.

It felt good to have fun with Keon. Usually we're at each other's throats. He would say something to me and I'd snap back, and from there it was over. But right here, right now, it felt nice to smile and laugh with him. It was sad to say, but I'd forgotten how this felt. I missed this.

After our huge breakfast, we actually started talking. The breakfast opened up a locked door between us. At first it was just silly things, but then it got a bit more personal.

"You think you in love with that nigga?" he asked out of nowhere as we kicked back in the living room.

"Why we gotta go there?"

"I mean, we here talkin' about some real shit, so let's get down to the nitty gritty." He sipped on some juice. "Do you think that you love him?"

"I don't think so. I know so."

"Ok, if that's what you want." He shrugged his shoulders.

"What happened?" I noticed the tension in his voice.

"Nothing." But I could tell that he was lying.

"What is it that you're not telling me?"

"Listen, as long as he makes you happy, that's all that matters."

"Well I am happy."

"Then that's what matters."

We spent the rest of the day talking. He told me some crazy stories about him and his friends. He also told me about some of the females that he dealt with. Some of them seemed as crazy as he could be sometimes, but I guess that was his type.

As the night approached, I asked him if he was going to go out. When he used to stay over at my place, he would just be gone. I would come home to find the spare bedroom empty. Now that he was injured, I had to make sure that he stayed home.

"Go out? You crazy. I'm going to stay my ass in here. If you need me, I'll be taking a nap." He surprised me and started walking towards the bedroom. Before he could close the door all the way, he turned to me and said, "Thank you for everything today. I really appreciate everything that you're doing Jayla." He smiled at me and went inside. Wow.

I didn't even have time to be shocked, because my phone started to vibrate. I looked at the screen and saw Darius's name.

"What?"

"I can't even get a hello?"

"No, you cannot get a hello. You are lucky that I'm picking up my phone, so what do you want?"

"All of that? What's with the attitude?"

"Don't act stupid Darius. What happened to you? You were supposed to pick up me and my brother up from the hospital."

"I just got back."

"Where were you?" I rolled my eyes. "Were you too busy with your wife?"

"No. Actually, I was with my divorce lawyer."

To hear that he was with his divorce lawyer made me smile. It was nice to know that he was actually trying to cut his ties with his bitch of a wife.

"Really?"

"Yeah. We were discussing ways for us to proceed with the divorce. I already signed my half of the papers."

"You have?" I was smiling now. He was really doing it.

"Of course. I told you that I was divorcing my wife, and I meant it. I was in his office all day. I guess my phone died. I finally charged it right now. As soon as I saw your messages, I returned your call. I'm sorry. I was so wrapped up in this divorce thing that I wasn't thinking of anything else."

"It's okay Darius." I sighed. "I'm just glad that you're doing this divorce."

"I'm sorry," he apologized again. .

"You don't need to keep apologizing again and again."

"I do. I love you, and I don't want you to think that I was trying to take advantage of you or anything."

"I know you're not," I reassured him. "I love you too."

"Let me make it up to you."

"I told you that it's okay Darius."

"I know that, but I just want to make it up to you, and I want to take you out. I miss you. It's been too long."

"Okay."

"How about we go get that steak you love?"

"At the restaurant by the Ritz hotel?"

"Yup, that same one. We'll get a room and you can have all the steak you can eat." He laughed.

"Shut up."

"I'll be there soon."

"I'm getting ready right now."

Right as the call ended, I hopped in the shower and then went to put on my best lotion, my sexiest-smelling perfume, and threw on a hot outfit. I had on a tight jumper with strappy sandals. As I brushed my long black hair into a neat, high ponytail, I heard a knock at the door. I went to the door. When I saw Darius standing there smiling, any tension I had melted away. He looked so good in his black fitted suit. He was always dressed for business. It was hard to stay mad at a man that made a suit look so good.

"Damn, you are so sexy." He grabbed me by my waist. He kissed me hard and deep. I brought my arms around his neck. I could feel him put his hand on my ass. Next thing you know, we heard Keon's door opening behind us.

"Nice to see you back on your feet." Darius reached out to shake his hand, but Keon refused to.

"I can't really move my arm." He lied, because he was left-handed and could have shaken his hand if he'd wanted to. I guess I should be glad that he didn't have an attitude. Had to count my blessings when I could.

"How are you feeling though?"

"I'm a little bit better." He had a bit of an attitude in his voice. When he looked at me, he softened his tone. "Thank you for asking."

"I'll be back later tonight," I told him while closing the door.

"Your brother seems more pleasant."

"He actually is."

We got to his car. He opened the passenger door for me as always. I was about to sit down when I saw a bouquet of yellow and white roses on the seat. I sat down and put the roses on my lap. Darius didn't have to do this. He must be really feeling bad. I knew that he wanted to pick us up, but if this meant that he was getting closer to being divorced, I already forgave him.

"Darius, you're so sweet." I leaned over and kissed his cheek as he buckled his seat belt. "I love it."

"I saw them and thought of you." He kissed me on the lips softly. "Are you ready to go?"

"Yup."

We were off. We got to the restaurant and I ordered the steak. Before it even got to our table, I was drooling. I didn't realize how much I had missed the steak. When it got to me, it was still sizzling. I smiled and looked over at Darius. He was smiling at me.

"What is it?"

"You are so beautiful, but you are gorgeous when you smile." My knees got wobbly when he said that.

"Thank you."

"After dinner, I'm going to show you how beautiful you are."

"Oh yeah?" I raised my eyebrow. "What are you going to do to me?"

"I'll let you guess."

The dinner was going great. It felt like old times. We were laughing and making eyes at each other. When we were finished, we couldn't wait to get to the hotel suite. We were making out in the street. He pushed me against a wall and grabbed at me, almost pulling off my clothes. The way he bit my neck, grabbed my ass, and had a tight hold on me almost made me forget that we were outside. It was late at night, so no one really saw us, but I had to restrain myself.

"Take me to the room," I begged as he slid his hand underneath my skirt. "I can't wait any longer."

From there, everything went at lightning speed. The door swung open, our clothes were off, and we were all over each other. I took him in my mouth fast and steady. When I tasted him, it was a sweet feeling. It felt nice to have him again. He gripped my shoulders as I sucked hard. His fingers dug into me, so I went harder. I started bobbing up and down on it. When he sighed, I start squeezing with my hands. I squeezed hard and sucked just as hard. I could hear him panting, and next thing I knew, he finished in my mouth.

"Damn," he exhaled. "You must have really missed me."

"You just don't know." I told him. I passed my hands all over his body. My fingers tingled just from touching him.

"Get on the bed so I can show you how much I miss you."

Once my back hit the bed, he dove his head in between my legs. He kissed all around before he started to lick my clit like always. The kisses made me quiver. It was like he was teasing me. When I felt his tongue touch me, I nearly jumped off the bed. He shoved his face in deeper, and I felt like I was in heaven. I couldn't breathe. His tongue movements were so fast and precise that he was making me so wet. I thought for one second that I was going to slide off the bed. All of a sudden he started to suck on my clit, and I lost it.

"Fuck!" I screamed, but he kept going on. I grabbed my boobs and squeezed hard. His hands pulled me closer to his face. I started to crawl away, but he wasn't going to let me go. Then came the rushes of feelings. I seized the bed and gave in to the feelings. I screamed loudly and exploded everywhere. I felt myself empty out on him and on the sheets. When I moved again, the wet spot was even damper.

"Ok, now let's have fun," he said wickedly.

He started to lick my breast. He squeezed and flicked his tongue around my nipple. He then started sucking on my nipple. He pulled at it with his teeth, and my breathing started to speed up.

"Fuck," I cursed again. "What are you doing?" I asked as he faced me.

"I want to kiss you." He grabbed me by the back of the head and kissed me deeply. My body was still quivering, and the way he kissed me, it was like falling in love with him all over again.

His hard penis was now pressing against my sex. He started passing it up and down my slit. The head was being covered in my wetness. He started to inch it into me, and suddenly he was in. He started pumping me fast and hard. We were slamming against each other. My body shook, and he looked at me intensely. I arched my back to take more of him in. He brought his body right on top of mine and started to rotate his hips. He moved around in me, opening me up.

"You started getting tight again," he mumbled.

"I haven't had sex in a long time." Which was obvious.

"Me neither." I wanted to ask if he was really being honest, but then he held up my legs and started to drive into me. I was moaning so loudly that I was biting my tongue. He had me screaming like crazy. We'd had great sex before, but this time was different. He must have really missed me.

He turned me onto my stomach. I propped myself up on my knees and arched my back. He slid inside me gently, but once he was all the way in, he was rough again. I fell against the bed. He held on to my hips and kept going. He reached and grabbed one of my breasts. He pulled himself out slowly and then rammed all the way back in. I gasped and then climaxed right after.

"You keep cumming back to back, huh?" He fell into me and held his place. "You missed me?"

"You know I did." I moaned and then he smacked my ass.

"I missed you too." He sped up. He kissed between my shoulder blades. "I really missed you." He then grunted and fell over. He came.

We were quiet. We were both trying to catch our breath.

"So, you're going to be divorced soon, right?" I was smiling. "Is that what you and your lawyer said? How soon will it happen?"

"It's in the works. I am just going to continue to play my cards right."

"Play your cards right?" I sat up in the bed. I wrapped the sheets around my naked body. "What do you mean by that?" I continued.

"You know, do what I've been doing," he answered.

"What you've been doing?" I shot back.

"Yeah." He nodded.

"So you mean by staying with Shenice?" I spat in disgust.

"It's not like that," Darius replied.

"Fucking bullshit." I stood up.

My whole body got hot again, but this time it was for a different reason. Was he really going to continue doing this?

"Don't get mad."

"What the fuck am I supposed to feel Darius? You're talking about not getting mad, but you're still with your fucking wife. Do you even plan on leaving her?"

"You know I do."

"I don't know shit! I mean, when we first met, I didn't even know that you were married," I reminded him. I crossed my arms. "You're trying to string me along, aren't you?"

"You know that's not what I'm trying to do."

"Oh fucking bullshit Darius. That is exactly what you're doing. You are just going to be in the process of getting divorced forever."

"You do know that divorces aren't done overnight."

"Yeah. The divorces that take the longest are usually because someone is holding on."

"Shenice!"

"No. I think it's you!" I shouted.

The room grew deathly silent. He looked at me with hard eyes. We were both pissed off. He took a deep breath.

"I know you're upset," he started to say slowly.

"No. I am more than upset. I'm pissed the fuck off," I told him flat out. "Are you leaving your wife or not?"

"It's more than that."

"Are you leaving your wife or not? It's a simple answer. Don't give me some bullshit. Don't give me some long fucking answer. Have you filed divorce papers?"

"I can't just—" He stopped his answer short. "I told you that I signed the papers."

"But signing the papers is very fucking different than filing them. Did you file them?"

"No." He looked away.

"I didn't think so."

I threw off the blanket. I looked for my clothes and my shoes. I started to get dressed, and he was right behind me.

"Don't leave. Not like this."

"What the fuck Darius?" I turned around and poked him in the chest. "You must think that I'm a fucking idiot." I rolled my eyes and then stopped. "Wait, I am a fucking idiot because I'm still here with you." I shook my head. Why the fuck did I have sex with him again? He was just playing me, like Keon was trying to tell me earlier. I guess it's true what they say, everybody plays the fool for someone at least once.

After I was done getting dressed, I made my way to the door.

"Jayla, I don't want to leave it like this. I am going to leave Shenice. I don't love her. I love you. I'm going to start my life new with you. I promise you that." I turned to him.

"I can't talk to you right now. I'm in the wrong frame of mind," I told him truthfully. I knew that if I stayed there I would just say some more hurtful things.

"I have a headache. I'm going home." I said. He opened his mouth to speak again, but I shook my head. "We'll talk later," I told him, pressing my finger against his lips. He nodded his head and I left.

I left the suite. Downstairs from the hotel, I saw that they had cabs lined up. My headache was getting worse. I really needed to get home. Once the cab pulled up to my condo, I paid the driver and tiptoed to my bed. It was really late at night. I didn't want to bump into Keon. I didn't need him to tell me "I told you so." I didn't need that tonight.

The next morning, my loud alarm clock started going off, so I rolled over and turned it off. My headache was gone, but I still felt shitty. What was I doing to myself? Darius was right. Divorce didn't take days. Sometimes it took years because of all the property they have to divide up. Darius made a lot of money, so there was probably a lot of stuff to be divided. Now on top of him having a bitch wife, I was going to be giving him hell too? I was so fucking stupid. I had just slept with him again! Ugh, I should have known better. I should have been patient. I have to wait until he is completely mine.

I started to make a pot of coffee. I had to be at work pretty soon, and I needed all the energy that I could get. I sliced open a bagel as the coffeemaker started going in the background. Keon's bedroom door creaked open. He stepped out and looked at me. As soon as we made eye contact, he shook his head.

"What?" I asked him with eyebrows raised. "What is it Keon?"

"You still messing with that man after what he did the other day?" He shook his head again. "You can do better than that J; I know you can." His voice was sincere, but I didn't care.

"You really got some nerve. You need to worry about ya own damn business. How about this? Instead of telling me that I can do better, why don't you look in the mirror and do better for yourself?"

I expected an argument, but instead Keon shook his head and went back to his room. I guess he might be right about Darius. Keon knew what games men played, so he might have just been looking out for me. Nah. That was not it. He thinks he knows it all, but he doesn't know Darius like I know Darius. Once everything is done, even Keon will have to admit that Darius is a great guy. I just had to tell myself to be patient, remind myself that I was his girl and that bitch Shenice was just an obstacle that needed to be dealt with.

Chapter 2

Shenice

The strong smell of masculine cologne woke me up. I picked up my phone and looked at the time.

"Shit!" I cursed and jumped out of the bed. I went straight for the shower. I was getting too caught up in the moment. Where was my head? I was racing around looking for my clothes as I was putting on lotion. Jamar watched me with an amused look on his face. If I had the time, I would ask him what was so funny, but I didn't have any to spare. It had been two weeks since the last time we had sex. After the first time, I knew it wasn't going to stop, but damn, I thought I could at least keep track of the time.

I went to the mirror and started to apply some makeup. Jamar stood up. In the mirror, I could see his reflection. He was still naked. His perfectly sculpted body always turned me on, and this time it wasn't any different. I was still in a rush, but I couldn't get my eyes off him. As he threw his shirt on, we caught eyes. He walked over to me as I was brushing my hair back into place. He hugged me by my waist and started kissing my neck. I was getting warm again, but I couldn't give in to the temptation.

"When will this whole 'angry and concerned wife' facade end? When will we get the chance to be together? I'm ready for us to be out in the open." He kissed my cheek.

"Hang tight, because I thought we originally agreed to just have sex. You know, I thought it was supposed to be just a physical thing."

"I know that's how it started between us, but I'm not going to lie to you Shenice. I want more." His eyes told me that he was being honest and sincere.

"Let's just start by being patient and see how this goes."

"So basically you're asking for us to just have sex?"

"Is that a problem?" I gave him a wicked look.

"Not at all."

He turned me around and held me close. We swayed back and forth to no music in particular. His scent started to overpower me again. It felt too good in his arms. Jamar had that type of touch that made you forget about your day. All I had to do was touch him and I was under his spell again.

Jamar was a completely different man than Darius. Darius touched you and grabbed you like he owned your body. And while that was great, it was so different and refreshing with Jamar. He would at first touch me tenderly. Every part of my body excited him. Maybe it was because the sex was new, but the high I got from his body alone, it sent me chills and thrills. Jamar was this gentle lover. He would know when to switch from gentle to aggressive at the right moments. It was like constantly having your body on a roller coaster ride, and it was always a pleasure to get off.

Flashback:

The first time Jamar and I made love, it was right after seeing my husband fucking that bimbo in the backseat of the car. I knew something was off when I followed him, but I didn't expect to find him fucking in the back of a car like some horny teenager. There they were in the car in an empty parking lot, and I watched it all. It was amazing how he could look me in the eyes and just straight up lie to me. It was really insulting and disrespectful. One minute he was talking such bullshit about working on us and on the family, the next minute he was with that woman in the parking lot. So as soon as I saw that, I called Jamar.

I waited for Jamar at the restaurant. I didn't hesitate going to the bar. If there was any time when I needed a drink, this was it. I needed something strong. Once I was seated, I ordered a dirty martini. When I finished my second glass, I heard someone clear their throat behind me.

"Hey." I smiled when I saw Jamar. "What's going on?"

"Shenice, you called me, remember?" He sat down next to me. "What's up?"

"I just thought that I should start out having a drink, but then it was magically followed by another." I sighed. "And maybe I'll follow it with another drink."

"Uh oh." He sat down next to me. "What are you doing drinking?"

"I'm of legal age."

"I meant that you know you're a lightweight." He laughed. "I thought you could only take white wine or some pretty mixed girlie drink."

"I did have a girly drink. It doesn't get more girly than some dirty martinis."

"No." He laughed. "A dirty martini is a woman's drink."

"You're trying to say that I'm not a woman?" I arched my eyebrow. "I assure you, I'm all woman. I just might be too much woman for people to handle," I told him. He chuckled and shook his head playfully.

"Can you handle me, Jamar?"

He coughed and started to choke. His eyes opened wide and looked at me bewildered. He started to gather himself.

"What did you say?" he said when he'd finished coughing.

"Come on Jamar, we're both grown." I touched his shoulder but he moved away.

"Shenice, what's going on with you? Are you really that drunk? You can't be that drunk!" He looked at me as if he was trying to see if I was sober or not.

"I'm not drunk. I may be a little tipsy, but I am aware of what I am saying." I sipped some more of my drink.

"Are you aware of what you're saying to me? Did you hear what you said? Do you know what you're doing?"

"I called you here, didn't I?" I touched his shoulder again.

"I'm not comfortable with this conversation." He looked away. I passed my hands to his thighs. They slipped to his crotch, where I felt a hard bulge.

"Oh hello. Someone is excited to see me," I purred, but then Jamar stood completely up.

"Shenice, I can't—"

"I know for a fact that Darius is cheating on me."

It was silent for a minute. In his eyes I could see that he was wondering what to say. As much as Jamar was a friend to me, I knew he was Darius's friend first. He had loyalty to Darius before me, and I got that. So I knew he was wondering if he should just come clean about all that his friend had done or just continue to lie to me.

"I don't know what you are talking about." He sat back down. He ordered a beer and avoided eye contact.

"I know Jamar." I told him straight up. "I know that Darius has been fucking around. You don't have to pretend that he's this faithful husband."

"Shenice, I don't know what you're talking about." Jamar was going to stick to this game. His loyalty to Darius was really apparent.

"Jamar, I saw him fuck her with my own eyes. He left the house out of nowhere. I followed him and I saw him get in a car and fuck this girl," I revealed.

Shock covered Jamar's face and then he shook his head. "She's some girl. I think her name is something with a J. I tried to find out more, but he never leaves his phone. I just remember hearing him say something to this girl, and he called her J. I think this is the same woman from before, but I'm not really sure." Jamar's eyes got soft.

"I know Jamar. You don't have to lie to me anymore. I'm not here to pull the truth out of you so I can go running to Darius. I already know. I know it all." I signaled to the bartender that I wanted another drink. "I know."

Jamar finished off his beer and then did something odd. He reached over and hugged me. His hold was soft at first, but then he squeezed me tightly. I wanted to resist it, but he felt so soft, and I was feeling so sorry for myself in that second. It felt nice to have someone feeling some sort of sympathy for me. I haven't felt this in a long time.

"I'm sorry," he apologized. "I'm so sorry."

"What are you sorry for? You're not the one that was cheating on me. I know that I may call you my play husband, but you're not my real husband."

"I know that, but I continued the lie. I should have told you the truth."

"You're his friend first Jamar, so I get that. I'm not mad at you for that." I patted his shoulder. "It just hurts to see it. He used to look me right in my face and lie..." I started to get teary-eyed, but I shook my head. I had promised myself that I wasn't going to cry over Darius anymore, and I'd meant it.

"You know what, you can't just be here drinking. As much of a lightweight as you are, I'm going to make sure that you're eating too."

"I'm not a lightweight." But I bursted out in giggles. "Fine, fine. We'll eat."

We were seated right after that. I ordered food and then added two extra drinks. Jamar just shook his head and ordered food without any drinks. The second my drinks came to the table, I started to go at them. Jamar reached over and picked up one before I could get my lips to it.

"What are you doing?" I reached for it and at the same time almost knocked down an empty glass.

"You already have had so much to drink."

"Can't I be drunk? Aren't I allowed to be drunk?"

"You are Shenice, but at the rate you're going right now, you're going to be really fucked up. How about you drink this drink after dinner? Let's let some of that liquor pass through your body."

"You are so caring."

"Thank you."

"And so nice."

"And again, thank you." He cut into his food.

I bit my lip, looking at him. Jamar was a really good-looking man. Now, I always knew he was good looking, but there was something extra...yummy about him. I couldn't quite put my finger on it. I felt myself get warm and excited. Uh-oh.

"So, what do are you going to do now?" Jamar asked, breaking up my thoughts. I just shrugged my shoulders.

"I'd be lying to you if I told you now that I had this planned. I don't even know where to start, to tell you the truth." I ate a bit of the food.

"I understand that. It can't be easy."

"It's not. My thoughts are all over the place, but there is one thing that I know."

"What is it?" He sipped some water.

"I'm just going to do what's right for my child."

"That's great Shenice, but..." he started, but then he drifted off. I kept waiting for him to speak some more, but when he started to dig into his plate again, I knew he wouldn't continue.

"But..." I led him back to his original statement.

"But don't forget to care for yourself. Your daughter will be fine, but if you're not in the right frame of mind, you can't serve her all that well as her mom. You need to take care of yourself, not for her, but for you too. You have to start doing things for you."

"You're right." I nodded. "You're absolutely right Jamar. I do have to start doing things for me."

"Good."

"Will you help me?" I brought the glass to my lips. "You know, do something for me?"

"Whatever you need me to do."

"I need you to fuck me."

Once again, he started choking. I sat there and watched him. When he finally composed himself, he looked at me with crazy eyes.

"You can't possibly be this drunk." He shook his head, but I laughed. "What?"

"You keep talking about me being drunk, and that's not even the case," I told him truthfully.

"To be honest with you, I am a little tipsy, but I'm not falling-over, make-stupid-decisions, regret-it-in-the-morning drunk," I informed him.

"So Jamar, when I ask you to fuck me, you can trust and believe that I'm not drunk and that I am 100 percent in the right frame of mind."

I went back to my food, although there wasn't much left.

"We shouldn't be talking about this."

"Why not? Like I told you earlier, we're both adults."

"But what about Darius?"

"Not for nothing, but fuck Darius. I've been faithful to that man for so long. Do you know how many times I get offers from men to have their way with me? I'm not some ugly housewife who lucked up by getting Darius. I'm fucking beautiful. I could have went fucking and sucking wherever I pleased if

I wanted to, but I didn't. I got dressed up in that priceless white dress, walked down an aisle, and made vows to that man and God. When I got married, every word I said, I meant them with all my heart, so I never cheated on him. My husband, on the other hand, he could never say that. So excuse me if I no longer give a fuck about Darius and his feelings."

Jamar's eyes went from shocked to understanding. He sighed, and his shoulders sank.

"I'm so sorry."

"Jamar, you have to quit apologizing. You didn't do anything wrong." He nodded his head. "But let's not beat around the bush anymore. Are you going to fuck me or not?"

"I can't."

"Why not?"

"Darius is my friend. I couldn't do this to him."

"How about we forego titles for now? Tonight I'm not Darius's wife and you're not his friend.

We're just two people who met at a restaurant, and then later they get a room and do what adults do." I smiled.

"But why me Shenice? I can't help but to wonder why me."

"Because right now you're the only man I can trust."

Jamar raised his hand. The waiter came over, and he told the waiter to get the check. I smiled even wider.

"So, we're going to do this then?" I let the busboy clear the table.

"Yes." His eyes showed me that he had something wicked in mind.

"Should we establish rules?"

"Rules to sex?" He chuckled. "Are you asking whether or not we should have a safe word?"

"No." I laughed. "Nothing that kinky. I was thinking more along the lines of what is this going to be between us. I think it should be just sex. I'm not looking for anything romantic."

"I wouldn't think you would be after all that has happened to you."

"Good...so just sex."

"Strictly."

Once we got to the hotel room, it didn't feel awkward. I was anticipating some sort of hesitation—after all, Jamar and I had been friends for years—but it didn't happen. As soon as we got to the hotel room, we looked at each other and we kissed. It scared me how natural the kiss felt. It felt like I should have been kissing him for all those years we were friends. When his hands started to slip off my clothes, I was so excited. I wanted him to touch me, wanted him to explore me, and I wasn't afraid for him to see all of me.

"Damn, you're so gorgeous." He spoke softly as I stood completely naked. He kissed my neck. "And you're so soft and smell so good." He licked my neck and kissed it right after. My body was tingling with anticipation. I was so nervous but ready for him. He knelt before me, opened my legs a bit, and licked me. I almost fell right there, but once I looked down into his eyes and saw how intently he was looking at me, it made me stand still. We walked over to the wall, and it helped with my balance. He had his tongue do curls, twirls, and twists, all inside of me. His tongue roamed inside my hole, darting in and out, making my knees weaker than they already were. I felt my legs start to shake, and pretty soon I had finished all over his face.

"Wow," he exclaimed.

"I'm sorry," I apologized. "I didn't know..." My head was feeling woozy.

"Didn't know your body could do that?" He finished my statement.

"Yes," I admitted. "What else can you show me?"

"You want more?"

"Of course. Unless that's all you can do."

"Now you want to challenge me?" he scoffed.

"I'm just letting you know you can do whatever you like."

"Whatever I like?" There was that wicked look again.

"Yes Jamar, whatever you like."

He started to peel off his clothes. He was down to his boxers, and I was mesmerized by his body. I reached out and touched his muscles. He pulled me close, and with one swift motion, he was inside me. I was in the air, pushed up against the wall, with him inside of me. I slammed my hands against the wall. I tried to hold on to him, but he was moving so quickly that my whole lower body was getting sore. Had I known we were going to have circus sex, I would have been more prepared. But he held on to me and moved into me like gravity wasn't even an obstacle.

"Damn it," I whispered, grabbing on to his neck.

"Don't cum yet. Lean back." He took two steps back. My body was leaning against the wall and was at an angle. I started to move my body like a snake against him. He hissed and then smiled. He reached for my breast and squeezed it softly. He then pinched my hard nipples, which caused me to shiver.

He walked me to the bed and we both fell against it. We were laughing, and he went back into me. He wiggled between my legs and pushed himself all the way in. I gasped, hugging him, and pulled his body tightly to me.

"How do you like it?" he asked me. "I know you say I can have whatever I like, but I like seeing you go crazy."

"Oh yeah," I gasped, because he was still moving his hips like crazy. My body was quaking. "It doesn't seem like you need any help from me."

"Do you like it fast?" He went fast. My whole body shook and vibrated along with his rhythm. "Or do you like it slow?" He slowed down and moved his hips around. I moaned out loud. "Thanks for that answer."

The way he rotated his hips was not fair. He hit my G-spot right on target with every other stroke. My legs were trembling and my toes were wiggling like crazy. I hugged him harder, moaned louder, and bit his shoulder hard.

"Fuck," he cursed.

"I'm sorry."

"Don't be. I like it," he continued, moving until I started to hear him grunt. He was almost there as well. I wrapped my legs around him and held on tightly. He started moving quickly, and the next orgasm in me was nearing as well. Just as he finished, I did too.

Present:

The first time we had sex was two weeks ago. From there we tried to play it cool, but here we were doing it again.

"I got to go," I told him after I finished fixing myself up. I took one last look in the mirror to make sure everything was in place.

"Back to go play wife." He didn't sound too happy. Not that I blamed him.

"That's not fair," I pouted. "This isn't easy for me."

"And it's not easy for me either." He took my hand and pulled me in for another kiss. I almost forgot that I was going, but I pulled away slowly.

"I know it's not, but don't worry. I have a plan."

Chapter 3

Shenice

I tried to sneak back into the place. I didn't want to wake up Darius. The last thing I needed was for him to come at me with a million questions.

"Hey." I heard his voice and it almost made me jump.

"Hi." I tried to keep cool.

"It's pretty late."

"Yeah. I know it is."

"How is she?"

"Huh?" I was in a bit of a trance.

"Your mom? How is she?" Darius asked. I sighed a bit in relief and opened my mouth with my ready-made excuse.

"I really don't want to talk about it, but she's feeling better."

"Oh, I get it."

"Yeah. You know she said that she wasn't feeling well, so I had to rush out to see her."

"So she is fine?"

"Oh yeah, she's fine. You know how my mom can be so dramatic at times. I got down there and it was like nothing had happened. I don't want to talk about anything that took me away from you." I walked over and kissed his lips. "Let's get back to our vacation."

After we'd come back from Jamaica and Darius was promising to be a better man, one of the things he said he'd do was make some more time for me. I, of course, thought that he was bullshitting, but a week after we got back he booked us for this romantic getaway at Lake Burton. It was this huge house with a spectacular view. I had to give my husband some credit for at least trying, but that all went to shit when I caught him fucking that girl in the car.

Once I'd seen that, everything had changed. I had sex with Jamar, and even as the date for our getaway to Lake Burton had gotten closer, I knew I had to have Jamar again. So Jamar had booked a hotel that wasn't so far away, and I lied to go see him.

The next morning Darius woke me up. He was so excited that it was almost weird. He was smiling and looked all too happy.

"What is it?" I was a bit groggy and still irritated from looking at his face.

"We are going on a little adventure." He was pulling the sheets off me. "Get up!" He then put a food tray over me. "I already make you breakfast."

"Oh gosh, is it going to be those greasy eggs that you always make?" I whined as I sat up. I looked down at the tray and was pleasantly surprised. "Wow, waffles! I love waffles." I smiled.

"Yes. I know this." He was sitting next to me. "So hurry up and eat. Then you're going to hop in the shower and get dressed."

"I got to choose my outfit first," I said.

"Don't worry. I already got that covered."

"You chose my outfit?" I swallowed hard. "I'm scared to look." I went back to my plate.

"I hung it right over there." He pointed to the other side of the room. I took my time to look at it. If it was some ugly, mismatched outfit, I wouldn't know how to feel. I finally turned over and I saw one of my favorite sundresses hanging on the closet door.

"Damn, you're getting it right." I smiled even wider.

"Give me a little bit of credit. I am your husband." He chuckled. "I think I know your style."

I hated when he did shit like this. It could make things so confusing at times. What were his intentions? Why was he being this nice and then cheating? I didn't get it. He'd been talking lately about having another baby, but then when his phone went off he would go into another room.

"Ok. I'll be ready soon."

After I scarfed breakfast down, I met Darius in front of the lake house. There was a car waiting. He stood there, dressed well and looking good.

"Are you ready?" He was smiling.

"Where are we going?" I crossed my arms suspiciously.

"I can't tell you that."

"You mean that you won't tell me that."

"Listen, can you just get into the car?" He laughed and held the backseat passenger door open. "We don't want to keep the driver waiting."

"Oh, since you care about the driver, why don't both of ya go to wherever?"

"Shenice, please..."

"Ok." I gave in and got in the car. His giddy self came around and got in on the other side of the car.

"Let's go."

When we pulled up to this beautiful restaurant, I was skeptical. I was glad that he was taking me out, but I didn't understand why he'd acted like I was about to walk on water. The way he'd come into my bedroom this morning, you would have thought Oprah was our cook. He opened the door and was smiling ear to ear.

"A restaurant?" I asked, still not getting the excitement behind his voice.

"I heard that this restaurant specializes in steaks."

"Okay..." I was still confused.

"Come on, stop acting like you don't like steaks."

"I like them, but I'm not crazy about them. Darius, you know I am crazy about pasta." I crossed my arms.

"Yeah, but you like a good steak too, so I thought that we could come here." He took my hand.

Dinner was great. Even with the past earlier confusion, Darius was sweet. He held my hand almost the whole time. He listened to my stories, and it was like he actually cared about what I had to say. After we finished eating, Darius all of a sudden wanted to be adventurous. We started going around to the cabins and houses in the area. We snuck out to the lake. We found this empty cabin.

"Come on. Let's go inside." He looked around the cabin. The lights were off, and it looked like no one had been in there for years.

"Darius, you're crazy." I told him. I kept looking around us, making sure that nobody saw us. Last thing we needed was to be arrested because they'd called the police on us.

"No one is in here." He went for the door, but it was locked.

"You see, it's a sign." I felt relieved.

"Come on, you use to like doing adventurous stuff like this."

"What?" I could be a big stick-in-the-mud, and I knew it.

"You remember." He nudged me, but I was confused. Then I remembered that he'd fucked that lady in a car. He probably was talking about her. Who knew where else they'd had sex? If she willing to fuck in a car, she'd probably let him fuck her in church.

"Can we just go back?" I snapped at him. He just nodded his head and led us back to our car.

I was in a pretty sour mood. I didn't want it to show, so I faked a smile the whole car ride back to our lake house.

"Can you get in the room first? I have to pay our driver," he said to me and I rolled my eyes behind his back. He was getting me madder. It was like nothing he could do made me happy.

When I opened the cabin door, a tear almost came down my eye. The whole place was covered with red and white roses, lit candles, and champagne bottles. It was so romantic. He'd even lit the fireplace. The whole thing looked like a scene from a movie. I sighed and walked farther inside.

"Do you like it?" Darius asked while looking at me.

"How did you do this?" I asked him while I felt my anger slip away.

"I had someone come in here and set it all up. That's why I was stalling. They texted me telling me that they were running late. I didn't want us to come early and ruin it."

"So that was all for me?"

"Of course babe. Who else would it be for?"

He didn't have to move toward me. I ran up to him, wrapped my arms around him, and kissed him. I started pulling off his clothes and pushed him to the bed.

"Damn. You're being so aggressive. I like that." He smiled and reached around and smacked my ass.

"Shut up." I pulled my clothes off quickly and got on top of him. I leaned down to kiss him and rolled my hips on top of his. I felt him get hard against me, and that turned me on even more. He slid my underwear to the side and suddenly slid himself inside of me.

I sighed and then purred. We started moving slowly, trying to gain a rhythm. He held my hips hard and started to move it around. I held on to his body and slammed my hips against him. He grunted and started to lift me up, placing me on his face. I rolled my hips against his tongue. He pulled me deeper, and I gushed all over his face. That didn't stop him though. He just stuck his tongue inside me. He darted in and out, and once I lost all my strength, he put me on my back.

He used his knee to open my legs. He went right inside me and went fast. I moaned and held on to the headboard. I pushed my hips along to his pace. I loved when we moved at the same tempo. I guess after ten years you got to know the other person and you knew their moves. He started rubbing on my button as he pounded away at me. He flicked his tongue over my nipples and started nibbling my neck. I laughed as his lips tickled me.

Darius gave me a look, and I knew what that meant. I got on all fours. He went inside me and pulled on my shoulders to put himself deeper inside of me. He pulled my hair and groaned, and I threw it back against him. We collided against each other until we both finished off.

"I'm going to hate to go back home." I was lying on his chest. His heartbeat was starting to slow down.

"Yeah?"

"I don't want to go back to the real world." I looked at him. "I want to stay right here in our little love nest."

"It's going to be like this back home Shenice."

"It is?"

"Yes, it is."

"Do you promise?"

"I do." He smiled at me.

When we got home, I kept waiting for the other Darius to pop up. I kept waiting for him to be neglectful, but I was pleasantly surprised when he was not. He was either with me, playing with our daughter, or even working. He was still sweet. When he kissed me, I almost had to open my eyes to make sure that it was him. It seemed like he was changing.

"So I just put her down, and she is sound asleep." He came up behind me while I was on the computer. He kissed my cheek. "I also have a surprise for you."

"Is it another getaway?" I teased, sticking my tongue out at him.

"Babe, we just got back. I do have to work sometimes."

"I know, but I just loved that place by the lake."

•

"Maybe we should look into getting a lake house."

"You're serious?"

"Completely. I'd like for our whole family to be out there to be honest."

"So, what's this surprise?" I noticed his hands were still behind his back. He chuckled and took out a bottle of wine with two wine glasses.

We sat down by the fireplace. He threw a match onto the logs and started poking it until there was a fire. He came over next to me and poured out a full glass of wine.

"Whoa," I commented. "Are you trying to get me drunk so that you can have your way with me?"

"Oh, I wouldn't have to get you drunk so that I could have my way with you."

"That is true." I sipped some of the wine.

The fire was crackling against the logs. I rested my head against his shoulder. Could life ever be this perfect? Could he just want to be with me and only me? If he never cheated, we could have this every day. This was the life that I'd planned for us before all of this had ever happened.

"Can I ask you a question?" I turned to him. He nodded his head.

"What is it?"

"Would you ever leave me? Or have you ever thought about leaving me?"

"Where is this coming from?" His face screwed up.

"Just answer the question." I pushed further.

"Shenice..." he dragged out.

"Darius, stop stalling." I crossed my arms.

"Yeah, I've thought about it."

I didn't expect that. I expected him to bullshit me some more, but when the words came out of his mouth, I felt my chest cave in.

"What did you say?"

"I'm kidding. I would never leave you."

"Then why would you say that?" I moved away from him.

"I was joking." He was kind of laughing, which was pissing me off more.

"Well it's not funny," I fumed. My whole body was getting hot.

"I thought you would get it."

"Not funny," I repeated to him, but this time I was angrier.

"Come on Shenice, you know me and my sense of humor. I'm sorry for that." His tone lightened up, and I could see that he was actually sorry.

"Okay." I crossed my arms.

"But I could never see myself leaving you. I love you far too much. I don't want to just be a great husband to you but a great father to our daughter."

"But you are a good father and husband."

"Shenice, I can do so much more. You deserve so much more. I am going to do so much better by you, Shenice." He smiled. "When I think of all that you've done and sacrificed for this family, I realize how lucky I am."

As sweet as his words were, I wanted to curse him out, because it suddenly occurred to me that no matter what he said, I had to go by his actions. Darius had spent years cheating on me, and although he was physically here with me now, every now and then he would sneak off with this phone. Whenever I finally got to his phone, I would see that he was still cheating. I didn't have to guess that he was still with that woman. He had been trying to win me over, but it wouldn't work. I knew better now. I'm not going to go back to ignoring what he was doing anymore.

"What about you? Would you ever leave me?" he asked, but he was chuckling.

"You know I love you. I couldn't imagine my world without you." I said

He smiled in response, and when he looked away, I shook my head and whispered, with a slick smile across my face, "If you only knew what I really have planned."

Chapter 4

Jayla

It was time to go to work. I stretched and made my way to the bathroom. I was cutting it alarmingly close to being late. After my shower and getting dressed, I ran to the kitchen and made breakfast for myself and Keon. It wasn't the huge feast like I did when he'd first come back, but it was good enough.

"Keon, I left you some breakfast in the kitchen!" I called out to him on my way out.

Work was very productive. It kept my mind off of Darius. I just did what I always did when he drove me crazy: I became the best worker that my supervisor ever saw.

"Damn Jayla, I love it when you work so hard. That makes me able to take more breaks," Charmaine joked as soon as I got there.

"You know what that means right?" Kim laughed. "So, what's with Darius?" They both looked at me, but I didn't feel like sharing. I was tired, plus I didn't want them all in my business.

"Everything is really good," I lied. "I guess I just have a bunch of energy today. But enough about me. What's new with you guys?"

"Who should go first?" Charmaine got started. "Because giiiiirrrrrrrrrllll, when I begin to tell you this tea, I will not stop."

"Then I'm just going to say that I started to try dating again," Kim said, biting into her sandwich. "But nothing looks promising."

"Well, what are you looking for?" I asked.

"I'm just looking for guys that are going to be honest." Hearing that word made me shudder, but I played it cool.

"You're going to find someone Kim, but you got to be open. You're meeting all these guys, and the first thing you do is look for flaws. If you want to be with someone, you have to try to be accepting or at least have realistic standards," Charmaine advised.

"It sounds like you want me to settle for a fool. No thank you." She sipped from her water bottle.

"Whatever." Charmaine rolled her eyes. "So let me get into this tea.

"Okay, so I started messing around with this new dude. I met him by the bar, and everything was cool until I found out that he had someone else." She sighed.

"Another girlfriend?" Kim asked.

"A wife?" I asked.

"No no. Not another *woman*." Kim and I just exchanged looks. "That dude was so close to busting this pussy wide open, and then I find him kissing some dude by a Dunkin' Donuts. So now I'm taking a break from men too." Charmaine sighed. "And donuts too."

Kim and I broke out into giggles. After that story, my workday dragged on. When it was finally finished, I was drained. As I walked to my car, I took out my phone. I turned it on and soon saw that I had a voicemail from Darius.

"I know that we didn't leave on the best terms, but that doesn't stop me from missing you. I just think that you and I need to sit down and talk. So, I made reservations for us at the Starfish restaurant for dinner. Please let me know if you're interested. I still love you."

I smiled and got into the car. I put in my Bluetooth and started to call Darius back.

"Hey," I said as soon as he picked up my call.

"I've missed you so much." Darius already had me smiling wider. "I need to see you. I don't think I can go without seeing you for so long."

"I know. I'm sorry about the last time."

"No, you don't have to apologize. It has to be frustrating waiting for my divorce to go through. I have to put myself in your shoes, so I know it's not easy."

"No, I know that Darius. I have to be patient. If you said that you're going through your divorce, I have to wait."

"Thank you so much. Starfish is this high-end sushi restaurant that's on Peachtree, and I've heard great things about it. One of my clients told me it's one of the best places that you can go to. As soon as I heard about it, you were the only person I could see myself going there with."

"I can't wait." I was now giddy and excited.

"I'll come over to pick you up around seven?" he asked.

I thought about it but didn't want to hear Keon's mouth. He didn't like Darius at all, and although he'd been nicer, I knew he wasn't going to keep his slick mouth to himself. There was no need to add tension or to have an argument between them.

"No. How about I meet you at the restaurant?"

"Okay..." He sounded confused. "I'll see you later then."

"Yes."

"I love you."

"I love you too Darius." I said before hanging up.

I got home and immediately went to the bathroom.

"Damn sis. You're just going to run past me without saying nothing to me?" Keon called from the other room.

"My fault," I called out. "I'm just going to start to get ready to go out."

"Oh yeah? You hanging with the girls?" he asked.

"No. I'm just going to see Darius."

I hopped in the shower right after that. I didn't need to hear a speech. I just wanted to take a shower and head out to see Darius. As soon as I got out of the shower though, there was Keon, right outside the bathroom door.

"You're really going to keep doing this? You really going to keep letting yourself get played by this nigga?"

"You don't know him."

"I recognize game when I see it. He's playing you Jayla. You're smarter than this."

Keon kept going on, but I started to drown him out. I just started to get dressed to go out. I went through my closet, trying to find something sexy.

"You really here looking for something to put on for a man that don't deserve you?" Keon said from the living room. I found my killer, sexy red dress and had to look for my black matte shoes. Keon was still going on in the background about Darius.

I finished putting on my makeup and fixing my hair. I pressed it completely straight and loved how it finished my look. While Keon was ranting in the background, I pulled out my phone and ordered some pizza for him. I added all the extras that he loved and even added dessert with a drink.

"Okay, I'm out of here," I told him as I grabbed my purse. "I ordered you something to eat. I paid for everything and even took care of the tip, so all you have to do is take it. How's your arm feeling? Did you go to the doctor's today?"

"He said that it's looking better."

"That's good to hear. I'll see you later." I walked over to the couch and kissed the top of his head. "Goodbye."

Keon sighed and shook his head. "I just want you to be careful sis. I know you think I'm just here talking shit, but I want what's best for you."

"Ok. Bye Keon."

I left the condo, but on the other side of the door, I couldn't get his words out of my head. They kept playing over and over in my head. Was there a reason why I couldn't get his words out of my head? Was there a reason why Keon was worried? Maybe I should listen to what he was saying, but it was hard to do that. Not only did Keon not really know anything about Darius, but he didn't understand that Darius and I loved each other. We didn't mean to fall in love, but we did, and we were going to do everything we could to be together.

When I saw Darius waiting for me at the restaurant, all my worries melted away. It was hard to stay away from him. He was sexy and thoughtful. This was the side of Darius that Keon didn't get to see. But I knew that as soon as his divorce was finalized, Keon would be seeing more of Darius. Hopefully when he saw us together all the time, he'd see what I saw in Darius. When we were all a family, it would be enough for Keon.

"Damn. You are looking so sexy," he said to me as I came up to him. I kissed his cheek and looked him up and down.

"I was thinking the same thing." I smiled and he chuckled.

"Come on. Let's go." He took my hand and escorted me to the restaurant. After we were seated, he ordered a bottle of champagne.

"Are we celebrating something?" I asked as the waiter popped the bottle.

"Every day with you is a celebration." He smiled.

"You are so corny." I laughed.

"Actually, I'm so in love. So corny and so in love looks the same sometimes." He chuckled again. "You know that you love it."

"Whatever Darius." I laughed.

Dinner was so delicious. It was nice to see Darius. Not being with him actually hurt me, but thinking back to Keon's words, I had to be serious. I could be in love, but I didn't want to be an idiot in love.

"What are you thinking about?" he asked me.

I slightly shook my head. "You don't want to know."

"If I didn't want to know, why would I ask you?"

"What's going on with the divorce?"

It was quiet between us, which didn't surprise me at all.

"Do you think that you can't talk to me about this stuff?"

"I think it's a very sensitive topic for you," I said. "It's hard to know what I can say and what I cannot say about it."

"We can talk about it. I don't ever feel like you and I can't talk about some things, Jayla."

"Ok."

"As far as my divorce goes, things are looking great. It looks like everything will be smooth."

"You served her papers?" I asked.

"No. Not yet." He replied.

"Darius..." I rolled my eyes. "I want us to be together. Do you know that's all that I think about? All I think about is how we're going to be together."

"And we are going to be together Jayla."

"Then why haven't you served her the papers?" I crossed my arms.

"But she will be getting served soon. I sent them out, so from here on out, it's just waiting on her to get them."

"So it's happening?"

"I told you I'd do it, and I meant it."

I got up and leaned across the table. He met me halfway, and we kissed each other.

"I'm happy," I informed him.

"I know you are."

"Come on. Let me show you how happy I am." I gave him a seductive look, and his face showed me that he understood what I meant.

Chapter 5

Shenice

The smooth R&B music coming from my car radio was soothing me. My nerves were on the edge, but I had to calm down. I was in this huge empty parking lot with a mission in my mind. If I was going to do this, I couldn't punk out or turn away now. I took out my phone and called the number.

"I'm here," I told the person on the other line. "I'm waiting in my car, and you don't have to worry about guessing which car. I'm the only person here." I listened to what they said and just nodded my head. "I'll see you when you get here. Once you are here, we are going to discuss my plans." They agreed and ended the call. I listened to the music on my radio and then I heard a car engine come on.

On the other side of the parking lot, a black SUV pulled up. The backseat passenger door opened and he stepped out. I got out of my car and half waved to him. He reached into the car and pulled out a package. He handed it to me, and I immediately opened it to make sure everything that I requested was inside. I saw the opium, marijuana, and some cocaine. He got it right, but I shouldn't be surprised. With this guy's reputation, I shouldn't have expected any less.

"Here you go." I got out my purse and handed him a wad of cash. He thumbed through the bills. "It's all there, don't worry."

"I'm never worried, but I am always about my business."

"Okay."

"What was this other deal that you were talking about earlier?"

"You always get down to business."

"I told you I'm always about my business, and I meant it."

"Okay. I need you to take care of someone."

"Take care of someone?"

"Yes." I started smiling. "There is someone that needs to be dealt with."

"You know about me, right?"

"That's right."

"And you know that all I do is deliver packages. You know that's all I do."

"Okay..."

"So why are you here trying to add all this extra shit? You know that I don't assassinate or kill people. That's not what I do."

I paused. He must think that I'm an idiot.

"Just like how you're about your business, I'm about mine as well. Do you really think that I would be doing this type of shit with a person that I didn't research?" He looked confused.

"What, you think I pulled your name out of the yellow pages? You think I put in some shit on Google and just magically got to you? You have a reputation. Let's not pretend that you don't."

"You don't know nothing about me." He was getting defensive.

"Let's not play this game."

"I don't know what you're talking about."

"You know exactly what I'm talking about. The streets are always talking. Don't let the Chanel on me fool you. I know about you. I'm not one of these stupid bitches that you meet that don't know shit. I'm smarter than that. So like I said, I'm not going to play that game with you. I need you to do a job for me."

He started to open his mouth but just smiled. He shook his head and held his chin.

"You...you about your shit." He smiled.

"Thank you."

"I respect that."

"And I respect you, and that's why when I needed this done, I didn't go to no little boy. I came to the man."

"Is that right?"

"Correct."

"So, what can I do for you? Who do you got beef with?"

We started to go over the details. He gave me a price, and we shook hands to agree on it. I gave him a piece of paper. He glanced at it briefly and then put it away.

"You sure you know what you doing?" he asked before I got into my car. "Because the last thing I need is for you to talk about you wantin' to call it off."

"That's not likely to happen," I told him. "I already have my mind made up." He nodded his head and got into the black SUV. After it drove away, I started my car and made my exit.

On the drive home, I blasted some old-school R&B music. I got myself lost in the voices of the greats of all time. I gripped the steering wheel and sang along to the familiar tunes. Music could take you to a whole new place, and that's what I loved about it. Right now it was easing me. I let Luther Vandross's soulful voice take me away. I had a long journey ahead of me. I'd put some things into motion, and I couldn't take any of it back, not that I wanted to anyway.

When I got home, I wasn't surprised to see that Darius was missing. As soon as he said he had to leave for a business dinner, I knew that it was bullshit. I just smiled in his face and said that I was going to spend the night with our daughter. Five minutes after I heard his car drive off, I gathered my daughter up and dropped her off at my mother's. My mother was always glad to help, and I took it to my advantage.

Walking around this empty house sometimes made me sad. It was just now. Knowing for sure that Darius was still being unfaithful could hurt. But I was done with hurting. I was tired of crying and I was tired of feeling sad. Now I was going to do me. I was sick and tired of being treated like shit. I was going crazy. I had to buy gadgets just to spy on him. He's had me driving to hotel rooms looking for him. He had this other woman up in someone else's condo. I even caught him having sex with her in a parking lot. I was just tired of it all.

You know what the problem was with infidelity? After you'd been cheated on, everyone expected you to be the bigger person. They expected you to just forgive it all and work on the marriage. No one gives you a second to grieve. No one gives you a second to think. And when you got angry, people acted like you were being unreasonable. People acted like I was not allowed to be mad, or vengeful, or maybe even a little bit vindictive. I thought that when you got cheated on, you were allowed to act however the fuck you wanted, do whatever the fuck you wanted, and say whatever the fuck you wanted. When you got cheated on, I thought you were allowed to be a little bit crazy. I was allowed all of these things. So excuse me if I was being a little irrational. I think that after ten years of me being faithful, that I've earned it.

I walked in the bedroom and spilled the contents of the package out onto the bed. I needed to release some stress. I was too amped up and angry. I grabbed some of the marijuana and opium. I put the rest of the drugs away and hid them in my stash spot. I had this stash spot by the floor of the bathroom. I hid it underneath a mat. I took out some rolling papers and rolled up the marijuana with the opium. I opened up the window and sat by it. I lit it slowly and started smoking it right after.

The stiff muscles in my body started to loosen up. I was at ease, and it felt good to finally be relaxed. I was always on the edge of something, and it was usually Darius's doing. I inhaled some more and started to feel sleepy. I inhaled as much as I could and put it out. I kept the window open to get rid of any of the remaining smells. I ran back to my stash spot and hid the rest of it. My body was yearning for bed. As soon as I got to bed, I fell right to sleep.

Chapter 6

Trey

I got out of the black SUV. It had been a long day of dropping off product and making money, and it wasn't even over. I threw two stacks of cash to the driver and told him to meet back in time to do some more work. He nodded at me and drove off. I made sure that he was completely gone before I ran upstairs to get to work. I had to count all this money to make sure everything was right. I was cool with my driver, but I trusted nobody around the money, especially when I had to give it in later.

I put the key into my small apartment's lock. It wasn't much, but I liked it like that. A lot of niggas fuck up by makin' money and buyin' some huge house. That was a rookie move. When you make the most money, that's when you to be quiet. You had to have small places like this so that the police didn't suspect you. I could remember people acting like I should have had some sort of mansion by now, but I just shook my head. I wanted all my money to myself. The fuck I look like giving it to someone else? I only spent my money on a few things, and a new house wasn't going to be it. Now one day I might get myself a crib, but I don't see it happening anytime soon. I was just going to continue to stack up this paper and keep to myself.

I went to the bathroom to wash my face. I was 6'3 dark skin with a sharp haircut. I had no problem with the females, but I didn't like to keep them around me too much. Females were the number one reasons why men fucked up. When I got with a woman, I liked to fuck them and keep moving. I didn't need one to make me feel like I had to spend all my money on her. Besides, in this game, it's not hard to get a beautiful female. In fact, I've fucked a lot of gorgeous women because of the money that I was moving, but I was smart. I'd learned from other people's mistakes. I'd seen men making crazy money, and all of a sudden it dried up because the bitch that they were with got expensive taste. Or I saw them get locked up because the bitch that they're fucking with can't keep her mouth shut. I'd rather put two bullets in a bitch head before I let her put a ring on my finger or her hand on my wallet.

The sound of the money machine counting the money was like music to my ears. I remember when I was coming up in the game and how I was broke, but now it was like such a distant memory. The things that I did to get this money and keep this money, others won't do. Some people would walk away from some of the shit that I did, but I didn't. Not only because I didn't give a fuck, but because I could set the price however high I wanted to. I was the best at what I did, which was why I'm always in business.

I thought about what Shenice wanted. Normally I would never take out some assassination from a drug client, but she was smart. Shenice was definitely not like most of the women that I sold drugs to. She knew how the game worked and how to get to the right players. She wasn't scared, and she acted like she was down for whatever. When I told her that I respected her, I meant it. A lot of females didn't know how to handle themselves, but Shenice was definitely not one of them.

Now, she's given me a lot of information about this person that she wanted to get rid of. She hadn't told me how she wanted them to die, but that was okay. I liked coming up with that plan myself. I've been doing it for so long that I know that I had various options. I could either shoot them in the middle of the night and disappear, or I could poison their food. I might just break into their house and wait and act like it was robbery. There was so much to do. I liked to be thorough, because mistakes were how people got caught. I was one of those rare people who had never gotten caught, because I planned everything out for every last detail.

I started to write down a list of what I'd need. I needed to get some latex gloves and other things for this to go down smoothly. Shenice was willing to pay my price, so she was expecting the best. I felt sorry for this person that had done her wrong, but hey, it is what it is. I'm not losing sleep over it. It's all about the money anyway.

When I heard the money machine finish counting all the money, I saw that I had the right amount of paper for my boss. I ripped out a page my small notebook and started to count up all the other drops I had to do. My pockets felt a bit empty, so I better go hit the streets. Once I sell some of the product that I have, I'll have even more money. I put the money in a brown paper bag and threw it onto my bed. I started to get undressed and took a shower.

Sometimes after a long day, I had to unwind. My customers liked to get high to get away from it all, but I just took a long shower. I didn't have time to waste. I had to get back to the money. So a long shower was really all the time I had for myself. After I was finished, I threw on some clothes, grabbed the bag, and made it downstairs. Like clockwork, the black SUV pulled up. This guy was always on time. He was reliable, and that's why I kept him around me.

"We about to make some drops. You know where the places are," I told my driver as I got in.

"Yeah I do."

"Okay, let's go."

We hit the hood and I started to do my drops. I gave the street soldiers some products to sell. As much as I would love to sell it all myself, it was damn near impossible. We were making so much money and getting so much product that we had to have people out there pushing it for us. The guys that we picked were so loyal to us. When I dropped off the product, they gave me the money from what they sold so far.

"Hey, how's it going?" I hopped out of the SUV to greet them. "Money is good?"

"Yeah," they replied.

"People giving you any problems?"

"Nah. Ain't nobody dumb enough to fuck with us," one of them replied. I smirked at his attitude. He reminded me so much of myself at his age. He had that type of hunger in his eyes. You could see that he loved the streets and that he was loyal to the team. I was going to keep my eye on him. You never knew when you needed someone.

"Good. That's what I like to hear." I smiled and patted him on the back.

I reached into the SUV. I put my hand underneath the seat and pulled out an envelope. I opened it up and saw that it was all there. I always had a little stash in my car. I hid it inside the seat of the car. I pulled out some crisps $100 bills and hid it in my hand. I felt for the tiny slit and put the envelope back in the car. It was like it was never there. It was the perfect hiding place.

"Just to show you guys that I appreciate the business that you're doing..." I handed each one of them $600. "This is just a little tip. I know you gonna get paid soon, but why not give you even more? I like how you guys are out here making money. I never have any problems around here, and I know that's ya'll holdin' it down. Good looking out."

"That's what's up." My mini me's eyes lit up. "See, that's why I fuck with this team. They know how to treat their peoples." He smiled. His friend smiled too.

"Thank you," he finally said. "Thanks a lot."

"Yeah, thank you," my mini me said.

"Alright, so I'm going to leave you guys to get back to the paper." We all exchanged hands. Once I got in the SUV, they broke apart. My mini me and his partner went to different corners. My mini me watched the SUV. Before the SUV was completely gone, he waved goodbye.

"Where to now?" the driver asked me. There were so many places to go that sometimes we didn't know where to start.

"Where's the closest place?"

"Got a drop around Peachtree. It's around all them fancy restaurants and whatnot. Go ahead and go there." I instructed

"Ok. I got you." He nodded.

The car zoomed through the streets of Atlanta. As I started to get to the richer and wealthier neighborhoods, I started to laugh to myself. Some of the people who lived in these neighborhoods acted so stuck up. They thought that they were so much better than the people that lived in the hood. What was so funny about that was that most of my clients came from these rich neighborhoods. It was the rich people that kept me in business.

When it came to the lightweight drugs, that was mostly from the hood. The stuff that moved most in the hood was weed and crack. Every now and then someone would say that they wanted some cocaine, but that was very rare. But in these rich neighborhoods? In these rich neighborhoods, all the hardcore drugs went here. I've learned time and time again that it's the people you wouldn't suspect to be on drugs. I've had CEOs, big money makers, reality TV stars, local celebrities, and even some politicians. It was funny to find out who was a customer. I didn't judge them though. I was just in it for the money. As soon as I got paid, I was gone.

We got to Peachtree and I told the driver to stop, so the driver pulled up and parked the car. I hopped out of the Black SUV and grabbed the product. I started to make my scheduled drops. I got the money from the customers, and in exchange I gave them the drugs. I told the driver to wait while I went down the block.

"I got your back," he told me as he patted his pocket. He then opened his jacket and I saw his gun.

"That's good to know." I nodded. "Keep it close to you in case some shit goes down."

I walked down the block and started to make some drops. I met this one guy behind a sushi restaurant.

I leaned against the brick wall of the alley. I always met this client in the alleyway. If people saw him with people like me, his reputation would be ruined, but I didn't care. I only cared about the money.

"What's going on?" I asked as he got out of the restaurant. He made sure the back door was closed before he spoke to me.

"I'm good." He gave me the money. I didn't even have to go through it to know that it was short.

"Where's the rest?" I asked as I threw it back at him.

"What are you talking about? All of it is right here." I sighed and walked over to him. Without hesitating, I smacked him across the face. "What?"

"I'm not a fucking idiot. I'm only going to ask this one more time because I'm feeling fucking generous today. Where is the rest of it?"

He got up and went back into the restaurant. I didn't know why people liked to fucking try my patience. I didn't have time for this shit. Time was money, and I couldn't afford to be a minute late. He came back out and handed me a stack of money. It felt heavier than before, but now I couldn't be sure.

"Now look at this bullshit. Now I have to count it because you wanted to play games."

"I'm sorry," he apologized, but I wasn't hearing it.

"No. Now you take it out and count it out loud."

He at first looked confused, but when he saw that I wasn't joking, he started counting out loud. After he was done, he handed me my money.

"I still think this is short."

"But that's all that I owe you."

"Yeah, you paid for the product, but you didn't pay me for my time."

"Excuse me?"

"You heard me. You wasted my time out here. What? You think that you are my only client? I have money to make, and you here fucking with my business." I stared him down. "I need to be paid for that fact. Don't you agree?'

He didn't say anything at first, but then he nodded his head. He saw how serious I was. He went into his pockets and pulled out $300.

"That's all that I have," he told me. I looked at him and knew that he was probably telling the truth, but I still wanted more.

"I make this money easy. Three hundred dollars won't do shit for me."

"But I don't have anything else on me."

"You go in there and get my money."

"But that's the restaurant's money."

"That ain't my problem."

He slowly walked into the restaurant. I laughed. I knew he was going to do what I said, because he still wanted the product that I had. He knew that if I got mad enough, not only could I not give him the product, but kill him too. He wasn't having that.

The door opened slowly. He handed me a stack of cash. I counted it and saw that it was $1,000. I knew the restaurant had more, but I let it go. I gave him the package. Before he completely took it from me, I held on to it and looked him in the eyes.

"If you ever pull that dumb shit again, you're dead. I can promise you that," I told him. He looked afraid. "You understand?"

"Yes sir." His voice trembled. I pushed him and threw the package on him.

I walked to the front of the street. I passed by the restaurant. The sound of the door closing behind me caught my attention. I turned and saw a woman walk out of the restaurant. I started to make my way back to the black SUV when I looked back. The woman looked familiar. I looked closely and couldn't believe my eyes. It was Jayla.

She was wearing this tight red dress and black heels. She always knew how to dress. She may have looked a little different, but her body was still the same. She always was so beautiful. Jayla had that type of beauty that made you stop and stare at her. I always thought she was this gorgeous girl, and it was nice to see that she still was. I was about to say something to her, but when I started to move toward her, I saw some tall man come out. He kissed her on the cheek and she smiled. It was obvious that they were together. He took her hand, and both of them started walking towards the parking lot. That was when it finally hit me.

I reached into my pocket and pulled out the piece of paper. I looked at the picture and then back up at the couple. Shenice wanted that person dead? I was wondering who did Shenice wrong, but I guess I just found out.

"Ah, I guess you're the one," I whispered to myself, shaking my head. It's a cold world out there. They won't even see me coming. And if they do see me coming, I'll make sure that it's the last thing they see.

I walked back to the SUV and tucked the picture into my pocket.

"Come on, we have more business to get to," I told my driver. He nodded at me and then started the car.

Chapter 7

Shenice

I took a last look at myself in my car mirror. I looked great. My skintight jumpsuit left little to the imagination. I would never leave the house like this, but I wanted to surprise him. Just the thought of how happy he was going to be made me smile. I got out of the car and headed to his door. There were some guys across the way that saw me.

"Hey sexy!" they yelled at me, but I ignored them. All this that they saw was only for one person.

I knocked on his door. As the door opened up, his mouth dropped.

"Damn. You look—"Jamar looked me up and down. He stopped midsentence as he stared at me some more.

"Do I look good?" I asked, walking into his apartment. His eyes were stuck on my body. He still wasn't speaking, so I made my way to his couch.

"Aren't you going to close your door?" I held back a laugh.

"I'm sorry. I can't help it. You look so good." He came over to me. "So damn good." He stood me up and kissed me. "It's not fair."

"What's not fair?"

"You coming here dressed like that." He grabbed my ass and squeezed. "Do you think that's fair?"

"Well why wouldn't it be fair? It's all for you. If anything, it's not fair to anybody else."

He smiled and started to move towards me for a kiss, but I moved away.

"Let's wait on that." I moved away from him and walked back to the couch. I sat down and crossed my legs. "So what shall we do first?"

"I can think of a couple of things."

"Get your mind off the sex part."

"Can you blame me?" He smiled. "But, I made us some dinner."

"You cooked for me?" I felt flattered. "I never heard about you cooking for any of your other female companions."

"You can't compare yourself to them tricks. You're nothing like them." He smiled. "I tell you all the time that you're special and special to me."

Jamar was a sweetheart. He started to set the table. He lit some candles, and just when I thought it couldn't get better, he put on some old-school R&B.

"You trying to get into these panties, huh?" I smiled. "I love these songs."

"I know you do." His eyes twinkled. The candlelight highlighted his sexy features. It was hard to keep my hands to myself, because I wanted this moment to last forever.

He finally finished setting up the scene. He gently took my hand and brought me to the dining room. He pulled out my chair, and after I was seated, he pushed it in gently.

"You want red or white wine?"

"Do you have any Moscato? I'm in the mood for something sweet."

"Funny, I was thinking the same thing." He gave me knowing look. I giggled, and he walked over with a bottle. He filled up my glass to the very top. "You are always talking about how much I am a lightweight."

"Yeah?"

"So how are you going to fill my glass up like this?" I laughed some more. "What is it that you have planned for me?"

"I'm not asking you to chug it all Shenice," he told me, chuckling. "There's just no need to keep refilling your glass. So I'm going to need you to take sips."

"You're not in the mood to take care of me?"

"Oh, I'm going to take care of you, but I don't need you to be drunk. You being drunk would kind of ruin that." He smiled.

The dinner was delicious. I never knew that Jamar could cook. He was like this whole new person to me. Of course, I'd known him for years, but not like this. I'd often wondered about him though. When he would be around Darius, he was always talking about females. He wouldn't dog them out, or maybe he wasn't doing it in front of me, but he always had a whole bunch of them. I just thought that he was handsome and that was all that he had to offer, but all of this was new to me. He could cook, he was attentive, he was sweet, and he actually cared about me. Because of Darius, I was a little bit skeptical about him, but I was going to enjoy him for as long as I could; I deserved it.

"So how was it?" he asked as I was licking the fork clean.

"Can't you tell?" we both started laughing. "Damn, that was so good. I didn't know you could cook like that."

"No many people do." He grabbed all of our plates and brought them to the kitchen sink. I followed him, bringing any dishes that were left. "No. You take your sexy self and sit on the couch. I'll be right with you in a second." I laughed and went back to the couch.

I flipped on the TV and waited for him to finish washing the dishes. Once he did, he joined me on the couch. I was watching some reality show.

"I don't know how you can watch this crap." He sighed, sinking into the couch.

"To be honest, I don't really watch it for the story. I mostly get stuck on their hair and wardrobe. Plus, it's nice to get lost in someone else's drama and life."

"You know what I like to get lost in?" He was rubbing my thighs.

"What?" I gave him a wicked smile. "Tell me."

"Some basketball." He laughed and grabbed the remote.

"No! I was watching that!" I laughed while trying to get the remote back, but he was holding it away from me. "How am I going to find out whether or not the side chick and the wife meet?"

"What? What type of nonsense—"

"I wanna see it!" I managed to sit on top of him and grab the remote. "See, I win."

We were laughing and play fighting like teenagers. Of course, just like young lovers, it soon went from play to something more sexual. He sat me on top of him and I started to move my hips around. He was getting aroused by my movements, and I was getting excited as well. My tight jumpsuit let me feel everything as I grinded against him. His hands dug into me and he moved along with me. It was like we were having sex with our clothes on. I started popping my hips up and down. He was getting so hard that I thought he was going to break through his clothes. We couldn't take it any longer.

"Take me to bed," I whispered in his ear and then bit his neck.

He lifted me up with my legs still wrapped around him. His hands were right on my ass, and as soon as we got to the bedroom, he was tearing my clothes off me. He threw me onto the bed. He slowly stripped in front of me. After he was completely naked, he got down next to me on the bed. He kissed me softly at first, but once he got started, it quickly turned passionate. He grabbed me and moved me closer. He kissed my neck, my shoulders, my chest, and pretty much everywhere. He was taking his time with me.

"I've never wanted somebody so much," he whispered as he made his way down between my legs. He opened my legs slowly and kissed each of my thighs. He kissed his way down, and when he got to the center, he licked his way there. He started to plant kisses right on my button. I trembled then when he started to suck on it. I started to scoot away because it was getting to be a bit too much. Not only was he sucking on it, but he was moving his head so he just kept teasing me. I knew that at this rate I was going to cum soon. He flicked his tongue all over my holes and did it quickly, and soon I gave in to the feeling. I climaxed, and my body jerked up and down.

He came back up on the bed. With him towering over me, he put his stiff self inside of me. After he opened me up again, he looked in my eyes as he went in and out of me. With every stroke, he had this intense look in his eyes. He would look down at himself entering me and then curve his back so that he could force himself deeper in me. I grabbed on to the mattress and pulled. His pace and movements were driving me crazy. He was going slowly, but the way his hips moved, it was like he was dancing inside of me. They rotated and everything worked together.

Jamar put his hands on my hips and started to pump into me faster. I bit my lip, and just when I was going to scream, he slowed down again. He was right on top of me. He put his arms underneath me and grabbed my shoulders. He pushed into me deeper and started to rotate his hips again. I felt my body quaking, and I couldn't believe another orgasm was going to come out of me. I held my breath, and it felt like my heart was going to explode out of my chest. I grabbed on to him and hugged him tightly as the new orgasm went through my body.

Jamar wasn't finished yet. He put me on top of him and put his arms behind his head.

"Can you still move?" he joked and started laughing.

"I can move just fine." I started moving slowly.

"Oh yeah?" He grabbed my hips and started slamming me against him, but I couldn't take it.

"Ok! Ok!" I gave in, pounding against his chest.

"What's the matter?" he asked, but he already knew the answer. I could tell by the look in his eyes that he loved making me weak to his touch, but I wasn't going to give him the satisfaction.

I leaned back and held his knees. I used that to move my hips against him. When I heard his hisses and groans, I started to push my hips harder and faster. He held on my hips and started to bring my body up and down. I winded my hips around and he sat up. We grunted and moved against each other. He kissed me deeply, and I pushed him back down. I hopped up and down him. He started moving his hips with me and grabbed me. I grabbed my breasts and squeezed. He licked his lips and then pushed himself deep inside me. I fell against him, and we climaxed at the same time.

As we were cuddling and holding each other, he kept playing with my hair and smiling at me.

"What are you doing?" I whispered, moving more into him. He smelled so great and was so warm.

"I'm thinking about something."

"About what?"

"You and me. What are we doing?"

"Isn't it clear? We were fucking and now we're cuddling." I tried to make a joke, but he wasn't laughing.

"You know what I mean. I know our situation is crazy, but I want us to be together. I think I can treat you way better than Darius ever did."

"You already do."

"But I want more. I don't want us sneaking around like this. You're not a basic bitch and I ain't a side nigga either," he said, looking dead at me.

I never heard Jamar really curse or speak slang, so I knew that he meant it.

"I know."

"No, you really don't Shenice." He sat up. "I'm falling for you. I'm not going to lie and hide my feelings for you forever. If we're going to continue to do this, I want us to be out in the open. You know it killed me to follow you and Darius to Lake Burton, but I did it because it was you asking me. So I got a place nearby and I met up with you, and it was nice but I wanted more. You know I wanted to be the one taking you out around Lake Burton. I want to take you out to restaurants and not give a fuck about who sees us. I don't like this hiding shit Shenice, because what I feel for you is nothing to be ashamed about."

Jamar got right to business. He pulled at my heartstrings like no other man. Darius may have currently been my husband, but Jamar was my man.

"It's not easy," I told him. "I've been with him for ten years, and we have a daughter together."

"I know Darius is going to be in your life for a long time; I'm not dumb, but I just think that you and I should be together. You guys can learn how to co-parent. A lot of divorced couples have been through it, so you're not the only one. On top of all of that, you're with me. I won't leave you alone, so you won't be going through this by yourself. When I tell you that I see a future with you, I mean it."

I got up and threw a T-shirt on. He put on his pants and followed me.

"Are you running away?" He laughed behind me.

"No. Not at all." I assured him. "I just need something to drink."

"I got it." He took a bottle of white wine out and poured us two glasses.

We sat on the couch. I could feel Jamar staring at me. I knew he wanted answers.

"Jamar, we are going to be together."

"When?"

"I wish I could tell you the exact date, but I can't."

"So when are you going to file for divorce?" When I didn't immediately answer, he continued. "You just take one day and file for divorce."

"Just like that?"

"Just like that."

"But what about you?"

"What about me?" He looked confused.

"What about you and Darius? You guys have been friends forever. You and him are practically brothers. What do you think is going to happen when he finds out about us?"

"It's not going to be good."

"Not going to be good?" I repeated his words back to him. "It's going to be crazy. He's going to lose his mind."

"I know." He shrugged it off like he didn't care.

"What do you mean by that?" I shrugged my shoulders at him. "Don't you care?"

"Of course I care. Darius and I are like brothers, and it sucks what's going to happen between us once he finds out, but it is what it is. He's just going to have to take it like a man."

"And what about my daughter?"

"You know I love her. I'll help you raise her."

"So you're going to go from practically being her uncle to being her new father."

"First, she already has a father, and second, I love that girl, so hopefully she'll understand."

"She'll be so confused at first."

"And she'll have both of us to help her."

Jamar was like heaven sent. The way he was standing firmly was only making my feelings for him stronger.

"I'm ready for us. I'm ready for all that life is going to throw at us if it means that at the end of the day, you and I are going to be together. You and I together is all that matters to me. Once you and I do come out and be honest with everyone, we can take on anything else."

"I believe you."

"Good." He gave me smile. "I don't want you to think that I'm bugging you by asking about it, but I just really want to be with you. I don't like this. When I do this sneaking around shit, it's no different than me having sex with random girls at the club. I respect you more than that. We don't need to be hiding in hotels rooms or at my place. We're grown."

"You're right. I want to be with you too Jamar. Even though it looks like I'm playing with you, I'm not. You know how I feel about you. You just have to trust and believe me when I tell you that I have a plan."

"A plan?"

"Yes. I have a plan, and once it's all done, it's going to be me, you, and my daughter."

He smiled and kissed me. We sat on the couch and discussed our plans for the future. He was happy and I was too.

"So we just have to stay calm and be patient. As long as we stick to my plan, everything will be fine." I smiled at the thought of us finally being together. Jamar kissed my forehead and went to get more wine, leaving me alone to my thoughts.

Darius was about to learn that he had fucked with the wrong bitch!

~~~

**Find out what happens next in
His Dirty Secret Book 4! Available Now!**

His Dirty Secret 4:

When Jayla discovers that Darius isn't the only one stepping outside of his marriage, she wrestles with whether or not to divulge that information or keep it in her back pocket for the time being. After all, it's not like Darius is an innocent man. She's more concerned with who Shenice is spending her time with.

Familiar with Jamar, Shenice's other man, Jayla knows all too well how this will turn out if Darius finds out. Can she control her anxiety and make sense of it all before tragedy strikes?

Find out what happens next in part four of His Dirty Secret! Get Your Copy Today!